Editors: Ann Redpath, Etienne Delessert
Art Director: Rita Marshall
Publisher: George R. Peterson, Jr.

Library of Congress Catalog Card No.: 83-71189
Grimm, Jakob and Wilhelm; Fitcher's Bird
Mankato, MN: Creative Education, Inc.; 32 pages. ISBN: 0-87191-942-7

Printed in Switzerland by Imprimeries Réunies S.A. Lausanne.

FITCHER'S BIRD

JAKOB & WILHELM GRIMM
illustrated by
MARSHALL ARISMAN

CREATIVE EDUCATION INC.

ONCE UPON A TIME

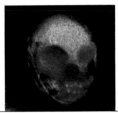

THERE was a sorcerer, who always disguised himself as a poor man and went begging from house to house in order to catch pretty young girls. Nobody knew where he took them, because they were never seen again.

Then one day the sorcerer came to the house of a man who had three beautiful daughters. He looked like a poor old beggar, and he carried a large basket on his back to hold the goods he was collecting. When he asked for some food, the eldest daughter held out a piece of bread. The sorcerer touched her, making her jump into his basket. Then he hurried away with long, strong steps and carried her to his house in the middle of a dark forest.

The house was splendid inside. He gave her anything she wished for, and said, "My love, I know you will be happy here with me, you have all that you desire."

Life went on like this for a few days when the man said, "I'm going away on a journey, and you will have to be alone for a while. Here are the keys to the whole house. You may roam anywhere, but take care that you never enter one room which this little key opens. I forbid you under pain of death." Then he gave her an egg and said, "Take care of this egg and carry it with you wherever you go. If you lose it, something terrible will happen."

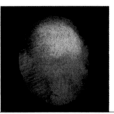

She took the keys and the egg and promised to do just as he said. When he had gone, she looked through the house, from bottom to top. The rooms glowed with silver and gold, and she thought she had never seen anything so grand. Finally, she came to the forbidden door. She wanted to go right by it, but her curiosity left her no peace.

She looked at the key, and it looked like the rest of the keys. She put it in the keyhole and turned it only a little bit, but the door sprang open. And what a sight did she see!

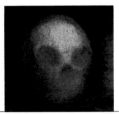

In the middle of the room a great bloody basin stood full of dead bodies that had been cut into pieces. Next to the basin there was a block of wood with a gleaming ax on it. She was so terrified that the egg she was holding fell out of her hand into the basin. She quickly took it out and tried to wipe off the blood. But it didn't help, for in the next moment the stain reappeared. She wiped and scraped, but the stain didn't come off.

Soon after the sorcerer came home from his trip, and the first thing he wanted was the key and the egg. She trembled as she gave them to him, and when he saw the bloody spots he knew she had been in the blood room.

"You went into that room against my wishes," he said. "So now you shall go into it against *your* wishes. Your life is over." And he dragged her in by her hair and cut off her head. Then he chopped her into pieces while her blood flowed all over the floor, and he threw her into the basin with the others.

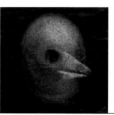

"Now I will go and get the second one," said the sorcerer. He went back to the house disguised as a beggar, and the second daughter brought him some bread. He caught her just as he had the first and carried her to his house. She did no better than her sister, for her curiosity led her to the bloody chamber. When he returned, she paid with her life.

Then the sorcerer went back and carried off the third daughter, but she was more clever. When he gave her the egg and the keys, she put the egg away in a safe place. Then she looked all around the house and at last went to the forbidden chamber. And what a sight did she see!

She found both her sisters,
cut into pieces, and scattered
in the basin. But she immediately gathered up the pieces
and put them together in the
right order—the head and the
body and the arms and the legs.
And when nothing was miss-
ing, the limbs began to stir with
life and the two girls opened
their eyes and were alive again.
They hugged and kissed and
were so happy.

When the man returned, the
first thing he wanted was the
key and the egg. He saw no trace
of blood on the egg, so he said,
"You've passed the test; you shall
be my wife." After that he had
no more power over her and he
had to do whatever she wished.

"Very well," she answered. "But first you must take a basket full of gold to my mother and father. You must carry it on your back. In the meantime, I will make everything ready for the wedding." Then she ran to her sisters who were hiding in a little room and said, "Now is the moment when I can save you. The evil man himself shall carry you home. But as soon as you get home, send me help." She put them both into the basket and covered them with gold so that no one could see them. Then she called the sorcerer and said, "Take the basket, and don't stop to rest, for I will be watching you from my little window."

The sorcerer took the heavy basket onto his shoulders and started off. But the weight pressed on his back and made sweat run over his face. So he sat down to rest. Immediately, one of the girls in the basket called out, "I can see you resting from my little window. Now get up and off you go." He thought it was his bride calling to him, so he started off. Again he thought he'd like to rest, but as soon as he sat down, one of the girls called out, "I can see you resting from my little window. Now get up and off you go." Every time he stopped, the voice pushed him on and he kept going until he finally arrived groaning and breathless with the basket of gold at the parents' house.

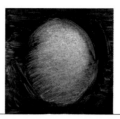

In the meantime the bride was preparing for the wedding and inviting all the sorcerer's friends. Then she took a grinning skull and decorated it with jewels and flowers and set it in the attic window, looking out. When all her preparations were finished, she jumped into a barrel of honey, cut open a featherbed and rolled in the feathers. She looked like a strange bird whom nobody would recognize as she left the house. On the way she met some of the wedding guests and they asked her:

"Oh Fitcher's bird, where
are you from?"
"From feathered Fitcher's
house I come."
"Oh tell us what the young
bride will do?"
"She sweeps full round the
house like new.
And look in the window—
she's watching you."

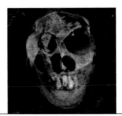

Finally she met the bridegroom, who came walking
back quite slowly. Like the
others, he asked her:

> *"Oh Fitcher's bird, where*
> *are you from?"*
> *"From feathered Fitcher's*
> *house I come."*
> *"Oh tell me what the young*
> *bride will do?"*
> *"She sweeps full round the*
> *house like new.*
> *And look in the window—*
> *she's watching you."*

The bridegroom looked up
and saw the decorated skull
and, thinking it was his bride,
he waved and acted friendly.
But when he and all his guests
had gone into the house, the
bride's brothers and relatives
who had been sent to rescue
her arrived and locked all the
doors. When nobody could
escape, the brothers set fire to
the house, and the sorcerer and
all his helpers were burned
alive.